15

JS 294.6

BENNETT, O.
A Sikh wedding

OXFORDSHIRE COUNTY LIBRARIES
SCHOOLS LIBRARY SERVICE

The author and publishers would like to thank the Singh family for all their help in producing this book.

First published in Great Britain 1985 by
Hamish Hamilton Children's Books
Garden House, 57–59 Long Acre, London WC2E 9JZ
Copyright © 1985 by Hamish Hamilton (text)
Copyright © 1985 by Hamish Hamilton (photographs)
All rights reserved

British Library Cataloguing in Publication Data
Bennett, Olivia
A Sikh Wedding.
1. Marriage customs and rites, Sikh——Juvenile literature
I. Title   II. Taylor, Liba
392'.5'0882946   GT2695.S4/
ISBN 0-241-11572-8

Printed in Great Britain by
Cambus Litho, East Kilbride

A SIKH WEDDING

Olivia Bennett   Photographs by Liba Taylor

Hamish Hamilton   London

It is the day before Pujenay's wedding. She and her sister Kuljeet show their little brother Munjeet a picture of the beautiful four-poster bed Mum and Dad are giving Pujenay.

Kuljeet holds up a coloured string with two knots in it. 'Can I untie the knot today?' she asks.

Pujenay's parents were given the thread by her future husband's family. It had five knots. Five days before the wedding Mum started to undo the knots, one each day.
'This is an old village custom,' explains Pujenay. 'It is said that the string helped village people – who didn't have watches or calendars – not to forget which was the wedding day in all the fuss and excitement.'

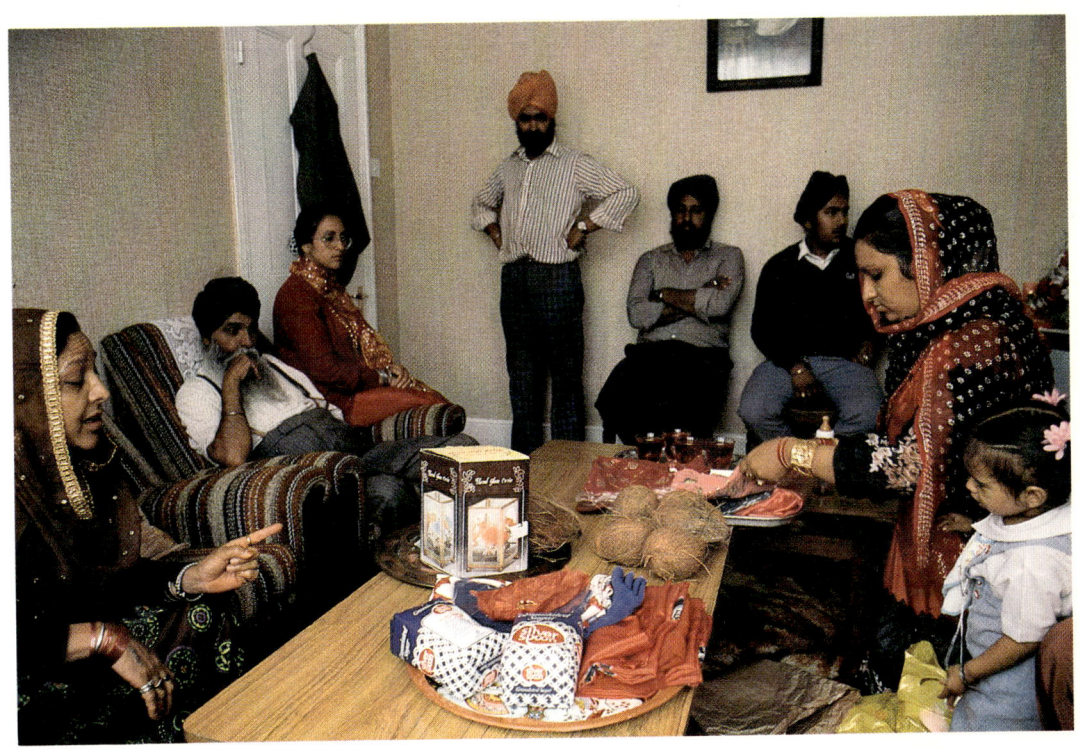

Downstairs, some more relations have arrived for the wedding. One of Pujenay's aunts unpacks the presents of coconuts, sugar and money which are often given to brides in India.

For several weeks, Pujenay and her family have taken part in various ceremonies to prepare her for the wedding. Today is particularly special. From now until her marriage, five 'bridesmaids' will stay with Pujenay all the time. Kuljeet is one of the bridesmaids. The others are all cousins. The five girls present Pujenay with some sweets. They untie the ribbon from her hair.

Outside in the yard, an aunt is drawing a circle on the ground. She uses a mixture of flour and water.

Then Mum places a piece of wood in the circle. Dad cut it from a fruit tree in their garden. He took off the bark and made the wood smooth and white. Pujenay steps onto the wood. This is to make sure her marriage will be fruitful and that she and her husband will have the children they want.

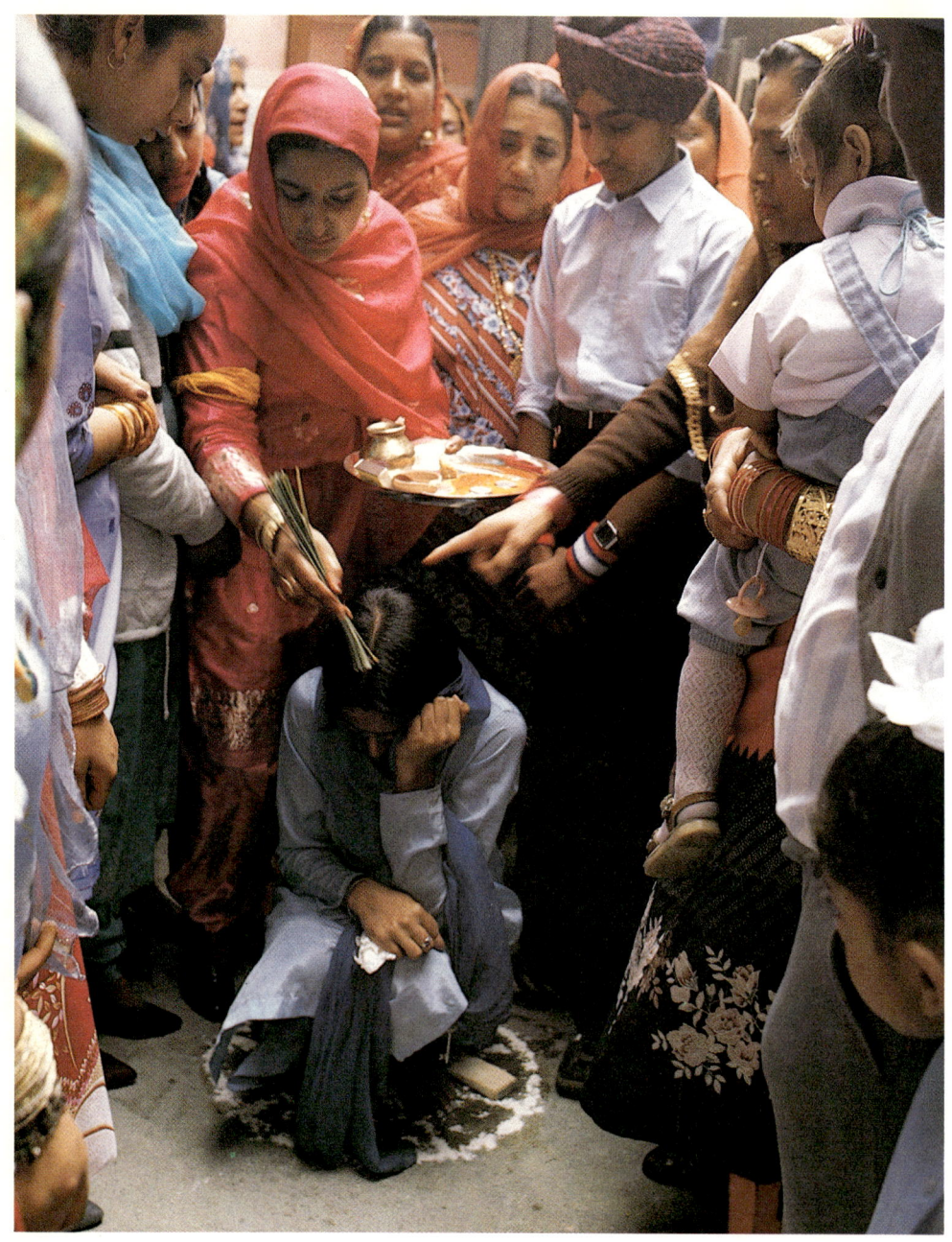

By now the house is full of relatives. The women crowd around Pujenay. They sing songs and take turns to brush some oil mixed with a herbal powder onto Pujenay's hair. This is to make her look a little scruffy before she turns into a beautiful bride. 'You're not supposed to make yourself pretty until tomorrow!' Kuljeet says.

Wedding ceremonies like these are Indian village customs which have been performed for hundreds of years. Most Sikhs come from Punjab, a state in northern India. Villages and districts often have their own local customs and ways of celebrating weddings.

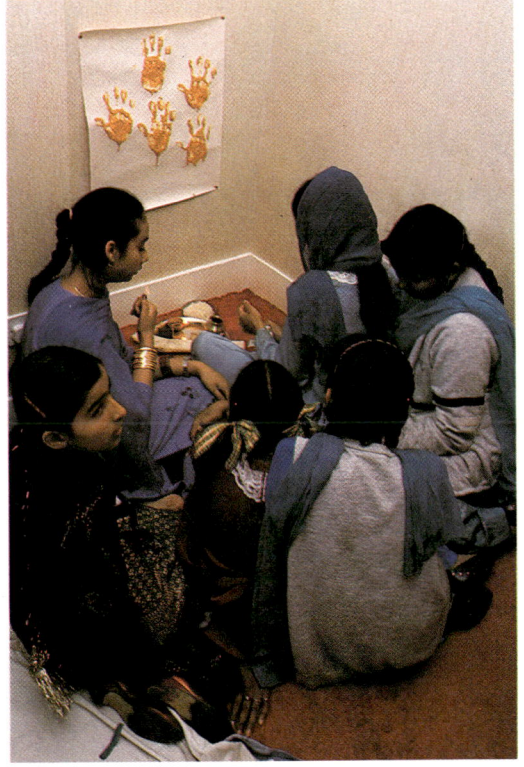

After this ceremony, Pujenay sits quietly for a while. Her five bridesmaids surround her. The five hand prints on the wall are to bring her good fortune. Five is a lucky number.

While Pujenay enjoys some peace, her father and grandmother hang a row of laurel leaves above the front door. In India, banana leaves would be used. They show that it is the wedding house. During the day, more aunts, uncles and cousins are expected to arrive.

In the early evening, Pujenay returns to the special circle. Several of her aunts hold a red silk cloth over her head. Mum kisses a silk scarf and touches Pujenay gently with it, as a way of blessing her daughter.

Meanwhile, other relatives are busy in the kitchen, chatting together and making delicious sweet pancakes. The first ones are given to Pujenay and the five girls. The rest are then shared by the whole family and their guests.

Everyone is in a happy mood. The women crowd into the front room. One of Pujenay's aunts plays Kikar's drum. They start singing Sikh folk songs. During each song, two or three of the women dance in the centre of the room. Clapping, singing and laughter fill the air. Pujenay watches quietly as her mother does a beautiful folk dance.

Later in the evening, Pujenay lies on a bed while her mother and aunts cover her hands and feet with thick brown henna. This is a paste made from oil and the crushed leaves of a plant. The henna will dye her skin a pretty, deep orange-red colour. Pujenay has to keep the henna on all night. Kuljeet and the other girls keep her company through the night.

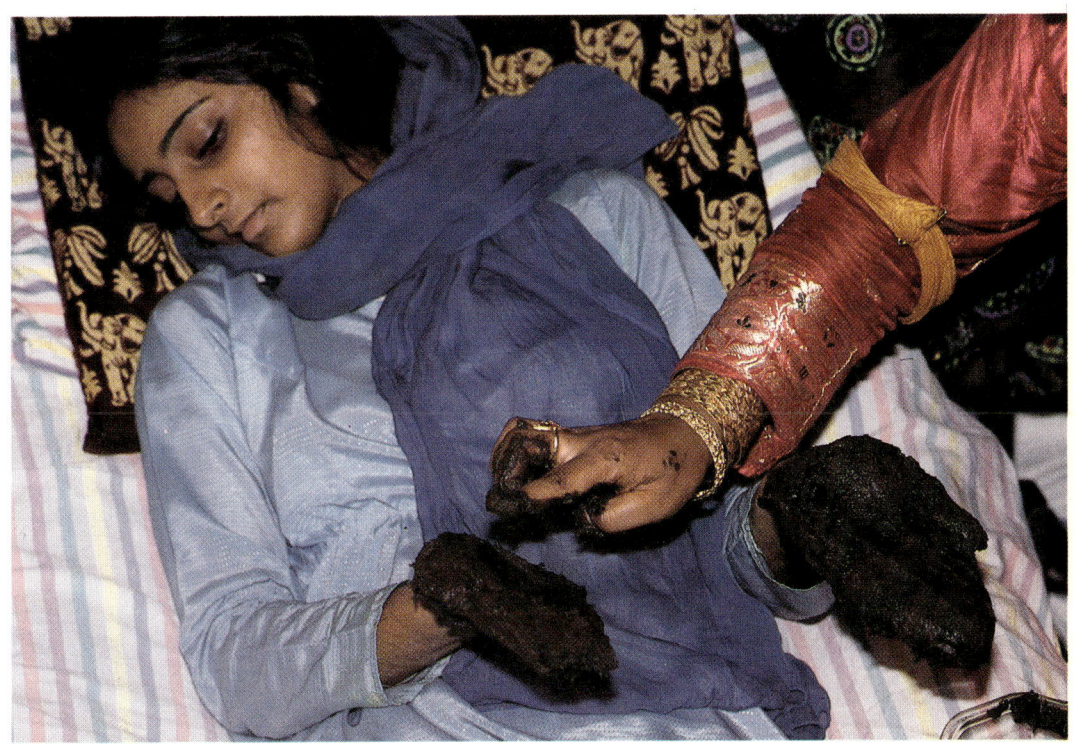

The day of the wedding dawns. It begins with Pujenay's uncle quietly singing some hymns. Pujenay looks quite different. For the last few days she had to wear the same tunic and trousers. At last she has been able to put them away, wash the oil and herbs out of her long shining hair, have a bath and rinse off the henna. She looks calm as she waits for her groom's family to arrive. She gazes peacefully at a little lamp. Its light is meant to make her beautiful like the sun.

Mum tries to make her eat some breakfast.
'I'm not really hungry,' says Pujenay.

Outside, her brother Butta and some cousins are waiting excitedly.

In the kitchen and the garden, other relatives are working hard, making lots of round flat pieces of bread called chappatis for the wedding guests.

'They've arrived, Munjeet!' call his cousins. Munjeet leaps off the swing and runs out into the street to greet the groom's family.

The granthi from the temple is there, dressed in white. He says a few prayers. The two fathers exchange money, rings and garlands. The groom's family and guests all wear yellow turbans. They have come by coach from Peterborough.

Pujenay's future husband is called Kalvinder. His face is hidden by a veil of flowers. He and his mother are welcomed inside. She presents the family with some gifts and jewellery for Pujenay. Then she and Kalvinder are offered sweets and a drink. Pujenay's mum ties back Kalvinder's garland of flowers. Kuljeet sneaks out to where Pujenay is waiting, to tell her how handsome her husband is!

It is time to do Pujenay's hair. Her granny weaves her shiny hair into lots of thin plaits. These are wound round into a pretty criss-cross pattern on her head.

Mum helps Pujenay dress and put on her wedding jewellery. The Pujenay covers her face with a red and gold shawl.

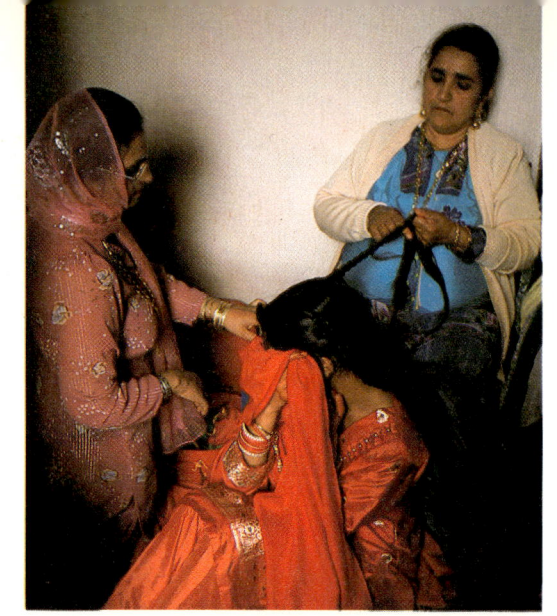

The groom's family wait at the temple. Pujenay's father-in-law is wearing a garland with a picture of Guru Nanak. Gura Nanak is the holy man who founded the Sikh religion and spread its teachings all over India. Guru means teacher or guide.

The granthi sits behind of the holy book of the Sikhs. He looks after the temple and reads from the book during services.

Pujenay arrives at the temple. She sits with her family, in front of the holy book. Pujenay's father gives her and Kalvinder a long yellow scarf to hold. This shows the link that will grow between them and join them together as husband and wife.

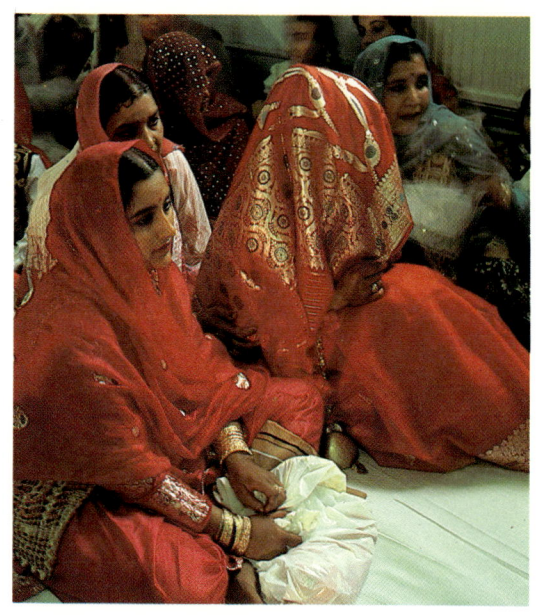

Kalvinder leads Pujenay around the holy book. When they have walked round it four times, they are truly married. Every important ceremony in a Sikh's life is done in the presence of the holy book. It is called the Guru Granth Sahib. It contains the teachings and prayers of the Sikh religion. It tells Sikhs to love others as much as God loves the world.

People sing hymns as the temple musicians play gentle music. Friends of Pujenay and Kalvinder make short speeches about them. Then they sign a register and the last prayers are said.

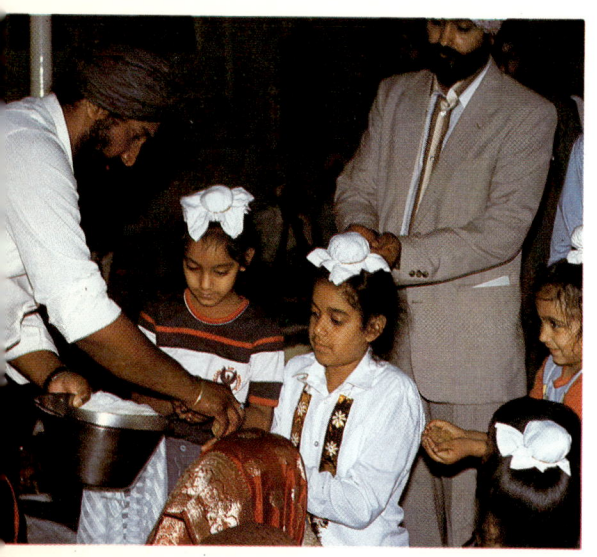

At the end of the service, the granthi makes some Karah Parshad. This is a sweet food made from flour and sugar. After the last prayers, everyone shares some of the Karah Parshad. It is a way of being given God's blessing and of showing that everyone is equal in his eyes.

When they leave the temple, the men go to a hall near Pujenay's home. They eat a delicious meal. There are meat and vegetable curries, salad, yoghurt, rice and chappatis – all prepared by Pujenay's family.

Everyone is very happy. They dance and join in the songs that some of Kalvinder's friends are playing on musical instruments.

Kalvinder's family have invited the Bhangra dance troupe to the celebrations. They perform a dance which retells an old Sikh story about a battle between good and evil.

23

Back home, the women sit outside and enjoy the wedding supper.

Mum starts to help Pujenay put on the rest of her marriage clothes and jewellery. She has gold rings, bracelets, anklets and necklaces. Loops of pretty twisted gold hang from her hair and cover her hands.

Soon Dad comes back from the hall with the other men. He holds his daughter close to say goodbye. Everyone feels rather sad as Pujenay prepares to leave her home and join her husband's family.

In the street, guests crowd around the wedding car. It is decorated with coloured garlands and streamers. Kalvinder gets in and waits for his bride.

Kuljeet will miss Pujenay very much. Rujney, her cousin, puts an arm round Kuljeet and comforts her. Pujenay's eldest brothers, Kikar and Butta, are going with Pujenay to look after her the next day. There will be some more wedding ceremonies and celebrations at Kalvinder's home.

'Pujenay will be back very soon to visit us,' Mum tells Munjeet. He feels sad to see his sister going away. But Mum smiles as she waves goodbye. She feels sure that Pujenay and Kalvinder will be happy.